ANIMAL LOOK-ALIKES

FROG OR TOAD?

By Rob Ryndak

Gareth Stevens PUBLISHING

Please visit our website, www.garethstevens.com. For a free color catalog of all our high-quality books, call toll free 1-800-542-2595 or fax 1-877-542-2596.

Library of Congress Cataloging-in-Publication Data

Ryndak, Rob, author.
Frog or toad? / Rob Ryndak.
pages cm. — (Animal look-alikes)
Includes bibliographical references and index.
ISBN 978-1-4824-2716-5 (pbk.)
ISBN 978-1-4824-2717-2 (6 pack)
ISBN 978-1-4824-2718-9 (library binding)
1. Frogs—Juvenile literature. 2. Toads—Juvenile literature. I. Title.
QL668.E2R96 2016
597.8—dc23

2015007000

Published in 2016 by
Gareth Stevens Publishing
111 East 14th Street, Suite 349
New York, NY 10003

Designer: Sarah Liddell
Editor: Ryan Nagelhout

Photo credits: Cover, p. 1 (background) Alan49/Shutterstock.com; cover, p. 1 (frog) Chros/Shutterstock.com; cover, p. 1 (toad) Hintau Aliaksei/Shutterstock.com; p. 5 Patryk Kosmider/Shutterstock.com; p. 7 (top) Savo Ilic/Shutterstock.com; p. 7 (bottom) Matej Ziak/Shutterstock.com; p. 9 (tree frog) Aleksey Stemmer/Shutterstock.com; p. 9 (fire-bellied toad) Volt Collection/Shutterstock.com; p. 9 (black-spined toad) cowboy54/Shutterstock.com; p. 9 (bullfrog) Chris Hill/Shutterstock.com; p. 11 (frog) Paul Reeves Photography/Shutterstock.com; p. 11 (toad) QiuJu Song/Shutterstock.com; p. 13 (toad) Aksenova Natalya/Shutterstock.com; p. 13 (frog) katatonia82/Shutterstock.com; p. 15 (top) Dirk Ercken/Shutterstock.com; p. 15 (bottom) Patrick K. Campbell/Shutterstock.com; p. 17 (top) Wollertz/Shutterstock.com; p. 17 (bottom) Erni/Shutterstock.com; p. 19 Auscape/Contributor/Universal Images Group/Getty Images; p. 21 (frog) Kuttelvaserova Stuchelova/Shutterstock.com; p. 21 (toad) Audrey Snider-Bell/Shutterstock.com.

Printed in the United States of America

CPSIA compliance information: Batch #CS15GS: For further information contact Gareth Stevens, New York, New York at 1-800-542-2595.

CONTENTS

What Is That? 4
Splitting the Difference 8
Body Type 12
Poison Pair 14
Interesting Eggs 16
What's in a Name? 18
Glossary 22
For More Information 23
Index 24

Boldface words appear in the glossary.

What Is That?

There's something hopping around on the ground. Is that a frog or a toad? Well, we're going to need to know more to figure that out. Let's find out the differences between a frog and a toad.

Toads and frogs are very similar animals in many ways. They're amphibians that belong to the Anura group of animals. Most frogs and toads start their life in water as a **tadpole.** From there, they grow legs and lose the tail that helps them swim.

FROG TADPOLE

TOAD TADPOLE

Splitting the Difference

There are more than 6,000 different **species** of frogs and toads. "True frogs" and "true toads" come from different animal families. How can you tell them apart? Scientists argue about this quite a bit!

RED-EYED TREE FROG
BLACK-SPINED TOAD
AMERICAN BULLFROG
FIRE-BELLIED TOAD

Most true frogs need to live near water to keep their skin wet. Their skin has a thin coat of **mucus** to help it stay wet. Most toads don't need water nearby to live because they have bumpy, dry skin. Many toads also have **warts**!

FROG

TOAD

Body Type

Toads usually have a wider body than frogs. Their legs are also shorter than most frogs, which means they hop differently! In general, the longer a frog or toad's back legs, the farther they can hop! Most toads take smaller hops because of their body shape.

TOAD

FROG

Poison Pair

Frogs are food for many animals. To stay safe, some give off a poison from their skin. Poison dart frogs are bright colors that tell predators to stay away. Many toads, like the cane toad, also have poison **glands** behind their eyes.

POISON
DART FROG

CANE TOAD

Interesting Eggs

Another way to tell frogs and toads apart is how they lay their eggs. Most true toads lay eggs next to one another, making long chains. Frogs lay their eggs together in clusters, or groups, that look like grapes.

FROG EGGS

TOAD EGGS

What's in a Name?

Toads can sometimes have smooth skin, and some frogs can live away from water. There's even a frog that lives in the desert! The Australian water-holding frog hides underground to keep its skin from drying out.

AUSTRALIAN WATER-HOLDING FROG

A toad can sometimes be called a "frog." And a frog can sometimes be called a "toad." Even more **confusing**, frogs can have warts, and toads can have **slimy** skin! Though you can't even trust their names, both animals are fun to learn about!

HOW CAN YOU TELL?

ANIMAL	"TRUE FROG"	"TRUE TOAD"
FAMILY	Ranidae	Bufonidae
WHERE THEY LIVE	often near water	often not near water
SKIN	smooth, moist	rough, dry, bumpy
BODY TYPE	narrow	wide
HIND LEGS	longer	shorter
HOW IT MOVES	high jumps	walk or take small hops
PREDATORS	many	not many
SHAPE EGGS ARE LAID IN	clusters	long chains

GLOSSARY

confusing: unclear

gland: a body part that makes something the body needs

mucus: a thick slime made by the bodies of many animals

slimy: covered by a sticky layer or film

species: a group of animals that are all the same kind

tadpole: the larva of a frog or toad

wart: a small, hard growth on the skin

FOR MORE INFORMATION

BOOKS

Beatty, Shannon, ed. *Frogs and Toads*. New York, NY: DK Publishing, 2014.

Kralovansky, Susan Holt. *Frog or Toad?* Minneapolis, MN: Super Sandcastle, 2015.

Rockwood, Leigh. *Tell Me the Difference Between a Frog and a Toad*. New York, NY: PowerKids Press, 2013.

WEBSITES

Frog & Toad

animals.sandiegozoo.org/animals/frog-toad

Learn more about frogs and toads at this San Diego Zoo website.

Frogs and Toads

allaboutfrogs.org/weird/general/frogtoad.html

Find out more differences between frogs and toads with this helpful chart.

Publisher's note to educators and parents: Our editors have carefully reviewed these websites to ensure that they are suitable for students. Many websites change frequently, however, and we cannot guarantee that a site's future contents will continue to meet our high standards of quality and educational value. Be advised that students should be closely supervised whenever they access the Internet.

INDEX

amphibians 6
Anura 6
Australian water-holding frog 18
body 12, 21
Bufonidae 21
cane toad 14
eggs 16, 21
legs 6, 12, 21
poison 14
poison dart frogs 14
predators 14, 21
Ranidae 21
skin 10, 14, 18, 20, 21
species 8
tadpole 6
true frogs 8, 10, 21
true toads 8, 16, 21
warts 10, 20